Friends

A Red Fox Book

Published by Random House Children's Books
20 Vauxhall Bridge Road, London SW1V 2SA

A division of The Random House Group Ltd
London Melbourne Sydney Auckland
Johannesburg and agencies throughout the world

Copyright © Rob Lewis 1999

3 5 7 9 10 8 6 4 2

First published in Great Britain by
The Bodley Head Children's Books 1999
Red Fox edition 2000

Printed in Singapore by Tien Wan Press (PTE) Ltd

THE RANDOM HOUSE GROUP Limited Reg. No. 954009
www.randomhouse.co.uk

ISBN 0 09 926612 1

Friends

Rob Lewis

RED FOX

Ambrose had moved to a new house with his mum and dad. He was sure he would make lots of friends.
"I hope they like swimming," he said.
"That's what I like doing best."

Ambrose met Clive. Clive was smelly.
He liked playing in the rubbish dump.
"I don't think he likes swimming," said Ambrose.

Zoe liked leaping about.
"Help!" cried Ambrose. "She's too wild for me."

HELP!

Maisie was playing the drums.
"Want to play drums with me?" she asked.
"No thanks," said Ambrose. "You're much too loud."

"Come and look through my telescope,"
said Charles. "I can show you all the stars
and I know all their names."

Ambrose didn't like anyone who
was cleverer than him.
"I'm not interested in stars," he said.

Bernie wasn't clever.
"D'you want to go swimming?" asked Ambrose.
"Wot's swimming?" said Bernie.
"Forget it," said Ambrose. "You're too stupid!"

Ambrose tried talking to Charlotte,
but Charlotte was shy.
In the end he walked away.

"Did you make any friends today?" asked his mum.

"No," said Ambrose.

"Why is that?" said his mum.

"There was nobody I liked," he said.

"Clive was too smelly,

Zoe was too wild,

Maisie was too noisy,

Charles was too clever,

Bernie was too stupid,

and Charlotte was too shy."

"Everyone is different," said his mum.

"If you want to make friends, you will have to join in with what they like doing."

"But I want to go swimming!" said Ambrose.

After tea Ambrose wandered off down the path.
He saw Charlotte looking through Charles' telescope.

He saw Bernie and Clive building a den in the rubbish.

He saw Maisie and Zoe playing music.

Ambrose was sad and lonely.
Maybe having friends was more
important than swimming.

So he tried making friends again.
He played ships with Clive in the rubbish.

He leapt with Zoe.

He built a train with Charles.

He helped Bernie with his spellings.

He played in a band with Maisie.

And he gave Charlotte a hug.
"You're my special friend," she said.
Then she gave him a big kiss.

All Ambrose's friends came to his house.
"What shall we do today?" they said.

"Go swimming!" said Ambrose.